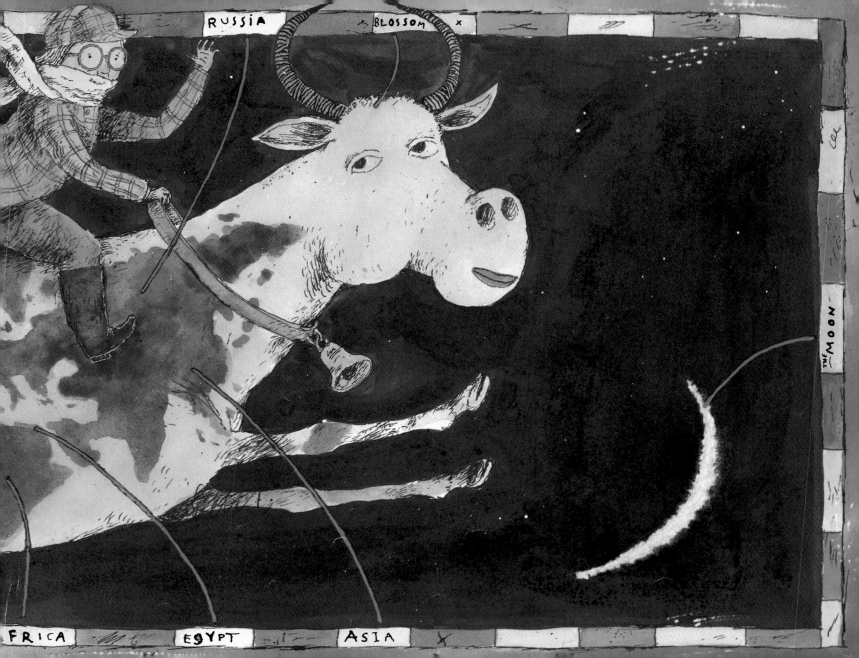

Santa Claus

DRESCHER

SHEPARD BOOKS

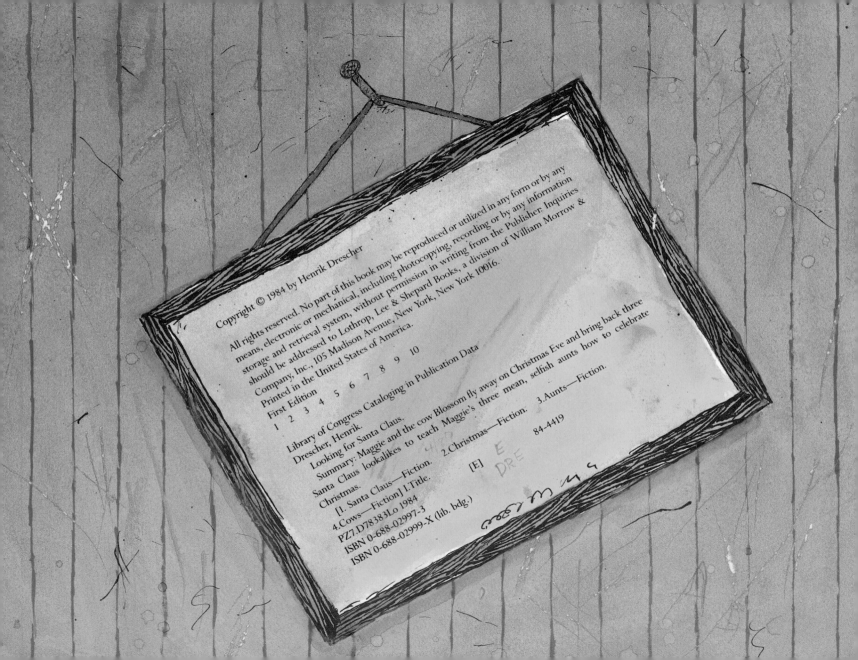

Library of Congress Cataloging in Publication Data

Drescher, Henrik.
Looking for Santa Claus.

Summary: Maggie and the cow Blossom fly away on Christmas Eve and bring back three Santa Claus lookalikes to teach Maggie's three mean, selfish aunts how to celebrate Christmas.

[1. Santa Claus—Fiction. 2.Christmas—Fiction. 3.Aunts—Fiction. 4.Cows—Fiction] I.Title.

PZ7.D78383Lo 1984   [E]   84-4419

ISBN 0-688-02997-3
ISBN 0-688-02999-X (lib. bdg.)

aggie's aunts hated Christmas.

They were mean and sour and loved to watch Maggie work.

On Christmas Eve, while Maggie cleaned, her aunts ate chocolates.

Before going to bed, she had to dig Blossom out of the snow.

Blossom invited
Maggie to go looking
for Santa Claus.
Away they galloped.

They flew over the moon

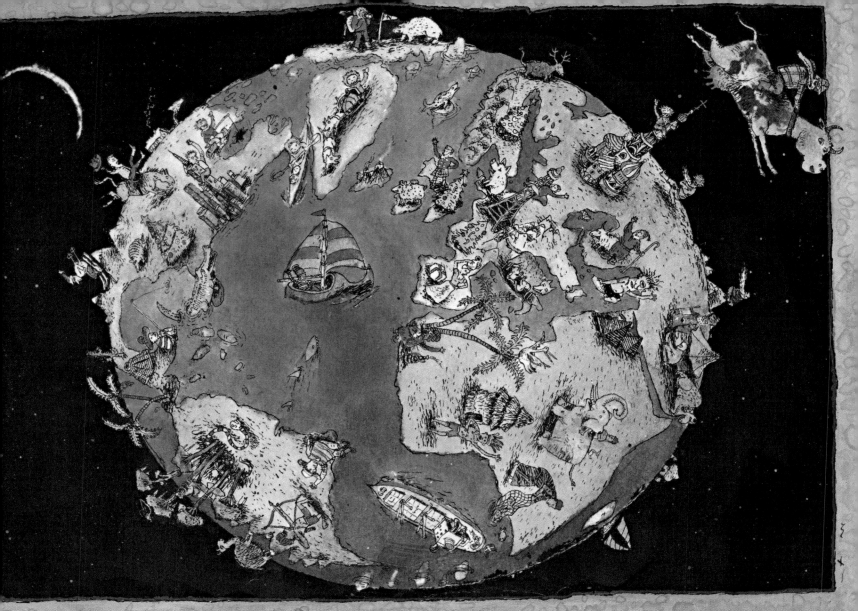

and around the earth.

In Russia, they discovered a lonesome cossack.

He looked like Santa Claus, but his name was Igor.

In Switzerland, a shepherd yodeled for help.

He looked like Santa with shorts on,

but his name was Frits.

In Egypt, a red-suited sheik was flying on a runaway rug.

He looked like Santa, but his name was Abdul.

Homeward they flew, across the Pacific.

Everywhere, people were celebrating Christmas.

Maggie's aunts were sending smoke signals for help.

Blossom's flight was smoother than her landing.

A path was cleared to the door,

and they were greeted with joy.

The aunts made
a Christmas feast.

Afterward, Igor danced
on the dinner table.

Then they all warmed their feet by the fire.

Suddenly, gifts tumbled through the chimney.

Everyone rushed into the night,

just in time to catch a glimpse of Santa crossing the moon.

THE X END

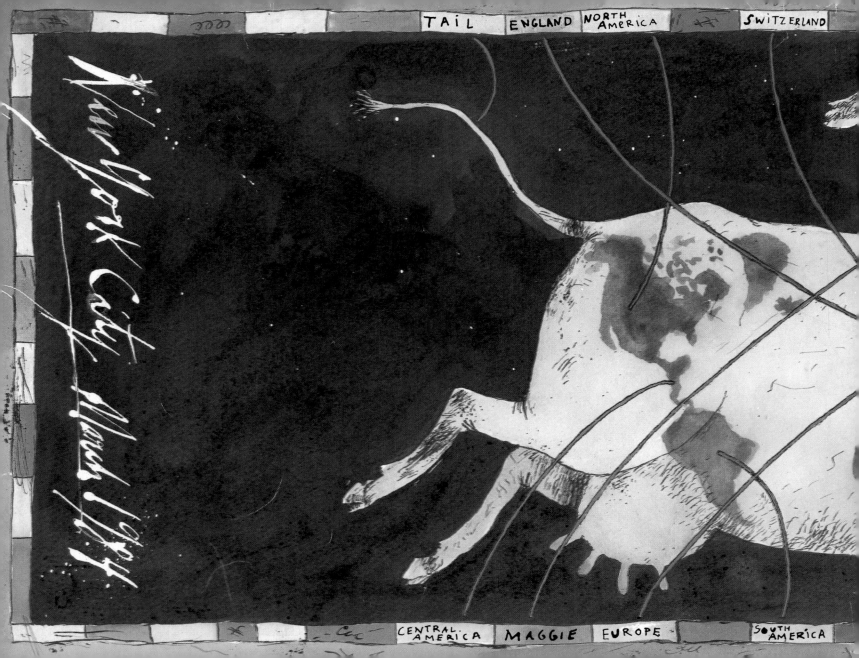